PUFFIN BOOKS

Sheltie the Hero

Make friends with

The little pony with the big heart

Sheltie is the lovable little Shetland pony with a big personality. He is cheeky, full of fun and has a heart of gold. His best friend and owner is Emma, and together they have lots of exciting adventures.

Share Sheltie and Emma's adventures in

SHELTIE THE SHETLAND PONY
SHELTIE SAVES THE DAY
SHELTIE AND THE RUNAWAY
SHELTIE FINDS A FRIEND
SHELTIE TO THE RESCUE
SHELTIE IN DANGER
SHELTIE RIDES TO WIN
SHELTIE AND THE SADDLE MYSTERY
SHELTIE LEADS THE WAY

Peter Clover was born and went to school in London. He was a storyboard artist and illustrator before he began to put words to his pictures. He enjoys painting, travelling, cooking and keeping fit, and lives on the coast in Somerset.

Also by Peter Clover in Puffin

The Sheltie series

Sheltie the Hero

Peter Clover

PUFFIN BOOKS

For Ben, Rod, Benjamin and Peter

PUFFIN BOOKS

Published by the Penguin Group
Penguin Books Ltd, 27 Wrights Lane, London W8 5TZ, England
Penguin Putnam Inc., 375 Hudson Street, New York, New York 10014, USA
Penguin Books Australia Ltd, Ringwood, Victoria, Australia
Penguin Books Canada Ltd, 10 Alcorn Avenue, Toronto, Ontario, Canada M4V 3B2
Penguin Books (NZ) Ltd, 182–190 Wairau Road, Auckland 10, New Zealand

Penguin Books Ltd, Registered Offices: Harmondsworth, Middlesex, England

First published 1998
1 3 5 7 9 10 8 6 4 2

Created by Working Partners Ltd, London W12 7QY

The moral right of the author/illustrator has been asserted

Filmset in 14/20 Palatino

Made and printed in England by Clays Ltd, St Ives plc

British Library Cataloguing in Publication Data
A CIP catalogue record for this book is available from the British Library

ISBN 0–141–30135–X

Chapter One

'Do you know where you're going yet?' asked Sally.

'No,' answered Emma. 'It's still a big surprise!'

'Is Sheltie going with you? I bet he is!' added Sally.

Sheltie pricked up his ears when he heard his name.

'Of course!' said Emma. 'Sheltie's part of the family. We're all going!'

1

Emma leaned forward and rubbed the little Shetland pony's thick mane.

Emma's dad was planning a special secret surprise for Mum. It had been Mum's birthday that week, and Dad was taking them all away for a short break somewhere as a birthday treat.

Emma and Sally had come home from school, finished their tea, and were now having a gentle ride with Sheltie and Minnow, Sally's pony. They were ambling along a bridle path on top of the downs, watching the clouds drift across the sky and talking about the special holiday surprise.

'This time tomorrow we'll be there, wherever it is,' said Emma. She could hardly wait to see Mum's face when she got back to the cottage. Dad had promised to spring the surprise before they all went to bed.

Emma was excited just thinking about it.

'How will you get there?' asked Sally. Secretly, Emma's best friend was wishing that she was going too.

'We're taking the car,' said Emma, 'and Mrs Linney is bringing the trailer over for Sheltie first thing in the morning.'

'I bet it's going to be the seaside,' said Sally. 'It might even be Summerland Bay again! You had a great holiday there, didn't you?'

Emma's eyes lit up at the thought of it. 'Wherever it is, it will be

3

fantastic,' said Emma. 'Dad's really good at planning surprises.'

Sheltie tossed his head in the air and gave Minnow a friendly nudge with his nose as if to say, 'I'm off somewhere special tomorrow!'

Emma and Sally made their way slowly back down to Little

Applewood. Then they went their own separate ways as Sally took Minnow home and Emma rode Sheltie back to the cottage.

'Have a great time!' called Sally over her shoulder as she waved goodbye.

'We will,' said Emma. Sheltie blew a noisy raspberry and Minnow flicked his ears back before answering with a soft blow.

Back in the paddock, Emma untacked Sheltie and settled him down for the night. Then she made sure that everything Sheltie needed for the weekend was ready to be loaded into his trailer the following morning. She measured out enough pony mix for three days into a sack, and put his special grooming kit into a holdall which Dad had hidden in the tack room.

When Emma skipped into the kitchen, both Mum and Dad were sitting at the table having a cup of tea. Emma's baby brother, Joshua, had already been tucked up in bed upstairs and was fast asleep.

As soon as Emma saw Mum she started to smile. Dad grinned too and gave Emma a special look.

'What's going on between you two?' said Mum. She could tell that they were both keeping something from her.

'Shall we tell her now, Emma?' said Dad.

'Tell me what?' Mum smiled. 'What are you two up to?'

Emma could hardly keep the secret in a moment longer. She felt that any minute she would blurt out the special surprise.

'Well,' began Dad, 'as a special birthday treat I'm taking us all away for a little holiday. You deserve a break, and it will be nice for us to go somewhere for a few days.'

'What a wonderful surprise,' said Mum. 'And how long have you known about this, Emma?'

'Oh, ages,' chirped Emma. 'But I didn't spoil it and say anything, did I?'

'No, you didn't.' Mum laughed. 'And I can normally tell when you're trying to keep a secret.'

'She's been absolutely brilliant,'

said Dad. Emma felt her face turn red.

'And where are we going then? Do you know that as well, Emma? Or is that a surprise to both of us?' said Mum.

'You'll both find out when we get there,' said Dad. 'And not a moment before. The best part of a secret surprise is making it last as long as possible.'

Emma couldn't wait for tomorrow to come. For once, she went to bed early without complaining, just so that the morning would come even quicker.

Chapter Two

The next morning, Emma woke to the
sound of the cockerel crowing in Mr
Brown's meadow. It was still very
early, but when Emma rushed to the
window and looked out she saw that
Sheltie was already wide awake too.

But he wasn't waiting by the
paddock gate this morning. He was
busy being fussed and petted by Mrs
Linney across the top of the wooden

9

fence. Sheltie used to belong to Mrs Linney and she was now a good friend of the family.

Mrs Linney had come to help Dad with his surprise and had brought along a little Sheltie-sized trailer. The trailer stood like a tiny house-on-wheels in the drive.

Emma threw open her bedroom window and called out to Mrs Linney. As soon as Sheltie heard Emma's voice, he looked up excitedly and did his funny stomping dance. Then he called to Emma with a loud 'good morning' whinny.

Emma dressed quickly and made her bed before rushing downstairs and out into the garden. It was time for Sheltie's breakfast.

'I bet you're really excited too, aren't you, Sheltie?' said Mrs Linney. 'I wish I was coming with you.'

After Emma had fed Sheltie, Mum and Dad came out of the cottage with Joshua. When Joshua saw Sheltie's trailer he realized that they were going somewhere and jumped up and down so hard that he fell over and sat down with a bump.

'Come on, Joshua,' said Emma. 'Come upstairs and help me pack.' She took Joshua's hand and led him inside.

When Emma had finished, Dad loaded all the bags into the boot of their car and then put Sheltie's things into the trailer.

Mrs Linney waited on the drive as

they set off. Sheltie stood inside the trailer looking through the little window at the front. Emma sat with Joshua in the back of the car and waved as they pulled out into the lane.

'Have a nice weekend!' called Mrs Linney. She watched as they disappeared up the lane.

'This is the best surprise ever, isn't

it?' said Emma. Her eyes sparkled almost as brightly as Sheltie's.

Mum reached back and ruffled Emma's hair.

'It's a wonderful surprise, Emma. And wherever it is that we're going it will be the best birthday treat I could possibly wish for.'

An hour later, Emma asked, 'Where *are* we going, Dad?'

'Not telling you,' answered Dad cheerfully. 'You'll all see when we get there.'

Emma and Mum smiled at each other. Joshua was fast asleep and strapped safely into his booster seat. Emma looked round and saw Sheltie peering through his little window.

'I bet Sheltie knows where we're going,' said Emma.

'I bet he doesn't,' laughed Dad.

Emma sank back in her seat and hugged her knees. She liked surprises. She decided to play a game and tried to guess where they were going.

'Is it Summerland Bay?' she asked.

'No,' said Dad, 'but I'll give you one clue. It's somewhere we've never been before!'

Emma laughed. 'That's not much of a clue, is it? How can I possibly guess where it is if I've never been there before?'

'Try harder,' said Dad.

Emma looked around at all the countryside they were passing

through. Flat open fields stretched away in every direction. 'Is it a farm holiday?' she asked.

'No,' said Dad.

'Is it a camping holiday?'

'No, but you're getting warm,' said Dad.

'How warm?' asked Emma, laughing.

'Very warm,' said Dad.

'It's a holiday camp, isn't it?' said Emma.

'It's not,' said Dad. 'But you'll find out soon. We're almost there.'

Up ahead, Emma suddenly saw the sea in the distance as they came over the top of a hill. The water sparkled like diamonds on a mirror beneath the blue sky.

Sheltie could smell the sea air as they headed down towards the coast, and Emma heard him whinny softly. Then suddenly Dad pulled the car over and drove up in front of a farmhouse.

'Here we are,' said Dad. 'Out you get!'

'Is this where we're staying?' said Emma. 'It *is* a farm holiday.'

'No it's not.' Dad grinned. 'Now, out you get!'

Then Mum and Emma both saw it at the same time.

A brightly coloured caravan stood in the far corner of the yard, with its two harness poles sticking out in front, resting on the ground.

'It's a caravan holiday,' said Dad.

'We're going to travel the countryside
and go wherever we like.'

Emma hopped from one foot to the
other. The caravan looked a bit like
Todd Wallace's old caravan, but
larger.

'Is Sheltie going to pull it?' asked
Emma. The caravan seemed far too

heavy for Sheltie. Emma was worried.

'No,' said Dad. 'We've got a special horse for that job.'

'A *horse*,' chirped Emma. 'Where? Can I go and look?' She was so excited.

'Yes,' said Dad. 'Just a quick look, Emma, and then come and help us carry things.'

Emma ran round to the back of the farm buildings and saw the horse in its stable. It was a huge brown and white carthorse, far bigger than Emma could ever have imagined. The name 'Toby' was painted on the stable door in green letters.

Emma raced back to the trailer to tell Sheltie.

'Just wait until you see Toby,' said Emma. 'He's a giant!'

Sheltie shuffled in his trailer and blew a snort as Emma helped Dad to lead him out.

Chapter Three

The farmer came over to greet them and they all stood and took a closer look at the caravan. It was beautifully painted with swirly blue and green patterns.

There were red checked curtains above the half door at the back, and green checked curtains across the small window at the front. Inside there were a cooker, a table with two long bench seats on each side which could be made into tiny beds, and two bunks at the back.

Emma tethered Sheltie to a ring on the side of the caravan and helped to carry things inside. Dad brought the cases, then went with the farmer to fetch Toby.

When Sheltie saw Toby his ears pricked up straight away. The carthorse towered above the little Shetland pony. Sheltie looked up with his big brown eyes and raised one hoof. Toby looked down and blew softly through his thick lips. Then very gently he nuzzled the top of Sheltie's head.

Sheltie whickered softly and rubbed himself against Toby's huge legs. Sheltie had never seen such an enormous animal before.

'I think those two have made friends already,' said Mum. She held Joshua in her arms and lifted him high to pat Toby's shaggy neck.

'He's a real gentle giant,' said the farmer. 'A bit lazy, mind you. But a real old character. Quiet as a lamb.'

'But he's as big as an elephant,' laughed Emma.

Emma watched the farmer show Dad how to harness Toby to the poles, then she helped to store his hay and feed on hooks at the back of the caravan. Finally they were ready.

Emma held Toby's bridle and talked to him while she stroked his soft muzzle, reaching up to pat his enormous neck. Toby was so big she couldn't reach anywhere near his ears.

Suddenly Toby shifted position and looked round for Sheltie.

'Dad,' called Emma. 'He's moving!'

'Don't worry,' said Dad. 'He can't go far, the brake's on.' Dad took the reins and climbed up into the driving seat. Mum climbed up too and sat Joshua in between them.

'You can ride Sheltie and lead the way, Emma!' said Dad, smiling.

'This is brilliant,' said Emma as she quickly tacked up. 'Follow the leader. But you'll have to tell me which way to go!'

Dad waved his map and called, 'Straight on.' He pulled up the brake and jangled Toby's reins. The caravan rolled forward.

Emma was glowing with pride as Sheltie walked on, leading Toby down the country lanes. The sun shone brightly and a gentle breeze blew Sheltie's long mane out to the side.

Toby couldn't take his eyes off his new little friend. And if Sheltie stopped for a moment, then Toby stopped too. When Sheltie blew a snort, Toby answered with a deep blow.

'They are funny, aren't they?' said Mum, laughing. Emma giggled and leaned forward to give Sheltie a kiss.

Dad handled the driving really well, especially as he had been given only a quick five-minute lesson by the farmer.

Then Mum had a go. Emma and Sheltie pranced alongside Toby. Sheltie was really showing off and lifted his hoofs extra high, like a

show pony. He was enjoying every
minute of this special holiday.

Although Toby was really strong
and could pull the caravan easily
along the flat, straight lanes, he was
very lazy. He kept stopping every

now and again for a sudden snatch of grass. That was when Sheltie helped by standing in front and blowing snorts to encourage Toby to keep going. But if Emma and Sheltie went too far ahead, Toby would stop again and refuse to budge until Sheltie came back.

'It looks as though Sheltie is in charge,' said Mum. 'It seems that Toby won't go anywhere without him.'

Sheltie on the other hand went everywhere that Emma asked him to, and was happy to trot just ahead of his new giant friend, leading the way.

When they finally stopped for the day, they made their camp in a beautiful spot overlooking the bay.

Emma asked if she could take Sheltie
for a ride.

'I won't go far,' she said. 'Just a
little way along to explore.'

But Toby hated being left behind.
Mum had to distract Toby with a
carrot while Emma led Sheltie away.

When they were far enough away,
she mounted Sheltie where Toby
couldn't see them.

The countryside was beautiful,
with cliff-top views across the bay.

Emma rode Sheltie for half an hour
and explored the first part of the next
day's route.

Dad had told Emma that in the
morning they were going to make
their way slowly down to the sea and
follow the coast road. And again
Sheltie would be leading the way.
Emma felt very important, just like
an explorer.

That evening, Dad hammered a big
peg into the grass and tethered Toby
and Sheltie on lead ropes to graze

while Mum made their tea in the caravan. Emma sorted out Sheltie's and Toby's feeds and scattered some hay on the ground. Then she gave them a drink in a plastic bucket which she filled from the caravan's water tank.

'It feels like a real adventure,' said Emma, peeping out over the half door to watch Sheltie and Toby. 'This is the best holiday treat ever!'

Mum agreed and gave Dad a hug.

They ate their tea and Emma was allowed to sit up late and watch the stars appear before bedtime. She couldn't wait to tell Sally all about it. She made sure she remembered every detail of the first day by going over it in her head at least three times before she finally fell asleep in her cosy little bed.

Chapter Four

The next morning started with a real panic. Emma woke to the sound of Dad's voice outside the caravan calling. 'They've gone. Sheltie and Toby have gone!'

Emma couldn't believe her ears. She leaped out of bed and rushed outside, still in her pyjamas. Joshua stayed tucked up in bed, sleeping.

Dad stood scratching his head,

staring at the spot where the big wooden peg had been. But the peg that Sheltie and Toby had been tethered to was gone. And so were Sheltie and Toby.

'Oh no!' said Emma. She was really worried. 'Sheltie! Where's Sheltie? What's happened?' Emma frantically looked around, hoping to catch sight of her little Shetland pony.

But neither Sheltie nor Toby was anywhere to be seen. 'Where could they be?' cried Emma. There were no gates or hedges to keep them in. Just the heathland stretching away as far as Emma could see.

'They must have pulled out the peg in the night and wandered off,' said Mum.

'But I hammered it in really well,' said Dad. He sounded so worried.

Emma felt sick. Her tummy turned a somersault.

Just then, Joshua woke and called from inside the caravan. Mum went in and lifted him out of bed. She stood on the caravan steps, with Joshua in her arms. Emma was close to tears now. She didn't know what to do. She looked from Dad to Mum in despair.

Then Joshua suddenly said, 'Sheltie!' and pointed down the road behind them with a stubby little finger. Emma spun round to look where Joshua was pointing.

There she saw Sheltie walking back towards them along the road. In his

mouth he held the wooden peg. And
on the end of the rope was Toby.
Little Sheltie was leading his giant
friend like a pet dog on a lead.

'Oh, Sheltie, you clever boy,' yelled
Emma. She ran with Dad to help
Sheltie bring Toby back.

'What would we do without Sheltie?' said Dad, ruffling Sheltie's forelock. Then he took the lead rope from the little pony and reached up to rub Toby's neck, reassuring him that everything was all right.

Emma threw her arms around Sheltie and gave him a long hug. Sheltie's breath tickled the back of Emma's neck and she found herself laughing. Sheltie pawed at the ground with his hoof and blew a snort at Toby as if to say, 'Now don't go off like that on your own again!' Then he looked around at everyone as if he was wondering what all the fuss was about.

Back at the caravan, Dad hammered the big peg in again, but

much deeper this time. Then he helped Emma with the breakfast feed for Sheltie and Toby.

Mum was already busy at the little cooker in the caravan, making bacon and eggs for everyone. Then they all sat at the table talking about their route for the day.

The caravan rolled along at a gentle pace. Emma and Sheltie led the way, and Emma talked to Sheltie. She told him where they were going and Sheltie's ears twitched as he listened to every word.

'First', said Emma, 'we're going to wind our way down to the coast road and stop for lunch at the Sandpiper Inn. Then we're going to follow the road which eventually leads to Bird Island. Isn't that exciting, Sheltie? A proper island. Not just half an island like the one at Horseshoe Pond.'

Sheltie raised his head and jangled his bit. He could already smell the sea and took a long sniff through his nostrils. Then he looked back to Toby and blew a snort as if to hurry him along. Toby answered with a deep whicker and quickened his pace.

'That's it, Sheltie,' called Dad. 'Keep him going.'

As the road levelled out on to the flatter coastland route they suddenly found themselves facing the sea, glimmering silvery-blue before them.

Sheltie stopped for a moment and watched the waves breaking on the sandy shore. Seagulls dipped and soared above the breakwater.

Emma stood up in her stirrups for a better look. 'Isn't it fantastic, Mum?'

Mum had to hold on tightly to Joshua, who was wriggling like a worm on her lap.

Bird Island sat like a magical mound rising out of the water.

'It looks like something out of a fairy tale, doesn't it, Emma?' said Mum.

'It's brilliant,' agreed Emma. She couldn't wait to get to the island and ride Sheltie along its magical shores.

Chapter Five

'Wait until Sally hears about this, Sheltie.' Emma sat back in the saddle and patted his rump. Sheltie danced on the beach. He liked the feel of the soft sand beneath his hoofs.

'Look at those two,' said Dad. 'They're really enjoying themselves.'

'We all are,' said Mum, and she gave Dad a hug. Half an hour later they stopped at the Sandpiper Inn.

The inn sat right on the beach and there was a good stretch of sand with patches of grass for Sheltie and Toby to graze.

Wooden tables and chairs were set out on the sand near by, in front of the inn.

A smiling waitress brought out sandwiches and drinks, and they all sat out on the beach and had lunch.

Toby closed his eyes and dozed in the warm sunshine. Sheltie stood close by and sheltered in the cool shadow that his giant friend made for him.

Emma drank her lemonade and stared out across the sea at Bird Island. She imagined that it was her very own enchanted island. And right in the middle on the highest point was her fairy castle with a smaller pony-sized castle next to it for Sheltie's stable.

'We'll sit here for a while,' said Mum. 'Joshua wants to play in the sand. Would you like to take Sheltie for a little ride along the beach, Emma?'

Emma didn't have to be asked twice. She had already leaped up and was calling to Sheltie. Sheltie's ears flicked to attention. He liked nothing more than racing along on soft sand.

'Don't go too far, Emma,' called Dad. 'And watch out for people on the beach.'

'Of course we will,' said Emma

over her shoulder. Then she urged
Sheltie into a trot.

Emma would have liked to ride
Sheltie straight across to her island.
She had read a book once where a
pony had swum into the sea with a
girl on its back, riding the waves. But
Sheltie didn't seem to be very keen

on actually going too far into the water. So they had a little paddle instead.

Then Emma rode along the wide stretch of beach. Sheltie needed no urging. He was off like the wind, galloping to the rocks right at the end of the beach. Then they galloped back and Emma felt as though they were flying on the wind.

'I went right along to the end,' yelled Emma.

'I know. We saw you,' said Dad.

'If it was a race you would have won a rosette,' said Mum.

'Sheltie, Sheltie,' laughed Joshua over and over as he bounced up and down on the sand.

An old fisherman had been

chatting to Mum and Dad about their
plans for the weekend.

'We're going over to the island,'
said Dad. He showed the fisherman
the road they were going to take on
the map. The road led to a causeway,
a long bridge which crossed a
shallow stretch of water across to the
island.

'You'll be quicker going across the
bay. Just here,' said the fisherman. He
jabbed the exact place on the map
with his finger. 'The tide will be out
until late afternoon. You'll have
plenty of time to cross.'

'Over the sands,' cried Emma
excitedly. 'I can't wait.'

'Are you sure it's safe?' asked Dad.

'Safe as houses,' said the

fisherman. 'Cars go across all the time. Wait for the tide to go out. Then over you go. Takes minutes. Ask anyone. It will save you ages in that caravan.'

'OK,' said Dad. 'Let's do it!'

'There's quite a way to go before we reach the bay though,' said Mum. 'We'd better get a move on.'

Chapter Six

They set off with Dad driving. Emma
rode Sheltie, and Sheltie showed
Toby the way.

In the distance, Emma saw the
causeway. She stopped Sheltie to
point it out to Mum and Dad.

Because Sheltie stopped, Toby
stopped too.

'Walk on,' said Dad, but Toby
wouldn't move until Sheltie did.

'I don't know who's driving here,' said Dad, laughing. 'Me or Sheltie.'

Sheltie blew a cheeky raspberry and quickened his pace.

'Come on, follow us,' yelled Emma, and everyone laughed. They reached the bay and the caravan rumbled down on to the beach, with the long stretch of sand before them.

The tide was right out and Bird Island looked only a short distance away. Toby stepped calmly on to the sand and with no hesitation followed Sheltie at his usual steady pace.

But Sheltie was so excited by the smell of the sea and the softer ground beneath his hoofs that he pranced about on the sand. Sheltie really wanted to race across to the island,

and Emma had to rein him in and keep him at a steady walk in case Toby decided to do the same. It would have been a disaster if Toby had broken into a gallop.

As Bird Island drew nearer and nearer, Emma felt that she was the luckiest girl alive.

The island turned out to be a truly

magical place. The golden beach disappeared away from the shore into rolling sand dunes which were topped with long grasses. Behind the dunes the island rose up through trees into a plump green mound.

On the top of the mound, in the very centre of the island, stood a huge grey rock. If you looked up at the rock from a certain angle, it resembled a bird sitting on a giant nest.

'Oh, look!' cried Emma. She was the first one to spot it. 'It looks just like an eagle.'

Dad parked the caravan and Mum helped Joshua down on to the sand. They all stood looking up at the big stone bird.

'That's why it's called Bird Island,' said Dad.

'Funny that you can only see it from here on the island's beach,' said Mum.

'That makes it even more special, doesn't it?' said Emma.

Just then they heard a rumbling noise behind them. As they all turned round they saw the back of the caravan moving away from them.

'The brake!' yelled Dad. 'I forgot to put on the brake.' Toby had wandered off, pulling the caravan behind him. Luckily Toby only went a little way before he stopped to drink at a stream that rippled its way down to the sea.

Dad ran over and caught hold of

Toby's reins. He tried to pull his head up out of the water, but Toby wouldn't budge. He was a very strong horse.

'Emma!' called Dad. 'Bring Sheltie over and get him to lead Toby back. Then we can find a nice spot to camp for the night.'

Emma rode Sheltie round in front of Toby. Sheltie seemed to know exactly what to do. He made pony noises to his new friend. And whatever the noises meant, Toby understood and did as he was told. He stopped drinking and let Dad lead him back.

Dad drove the caravan again, with Joshua sitting safely next to him. Mum walked alongside to stretch her legs. Emma and Sheltie led the way as usual, and they went off on a little tour of the island.

On the far side they found the ideal place to set up camp. Lush grass grew down from the hill and spread out like a soft green carpet on to the sands. It was nice and flat with a view across the bay to the headland. In a few hours the sun would start to go down and they would be able to watch it drop into the sea.

Dad hammered the tethering peg deep into the sand then set up a barbecue on the beach.

They cooked sausages on sticks for their tea, then afterwards played football on the beach. Sheltie joined in and chased the ball each time it rolled away down to the sea. Several times Sheltie accidentally kicked the ball as he ran. Then he learned that if he struck out with his hind legs he could send the ball flying out backwards across the waves.

'Oh, Sheltie!' said Emma. 'Don't be so naughty. We'll lose the ball.'

But Sheltie just tossed his head and blew raspberries. Sheltie liked this new game.

'He makes a good footballer though, doesn't he, Emma?' laughed Dad. 'I've never seen a pony kick a ball before!'

'Sheltie can do anything,' said Emma. 'But I wish he would kick the ball this way up the beach and stop sending it into the sea.'

Emma rolled up her jeans again and waded out for the ball for the third time.

They played for at least another hour before it was time to settle down for the night. Emma laid out

some hay for Sheltie and Toby. She
pushed the plastic bucket into the
sand and filled it with fresh water
from the caravan's tank. Then she
pushed in another bucket and
scooped in some feed. Toby put his
nose into the bucket straight away
and ate the lot in one go. Sheltie
looked on in disbelief.

'Don't worry, Sheltie,' said Emma.
'I'll give you yours now.' She fed
Sheltie then she clipped the lead rope
to his head collar and tethered him to
the peg alongside Toby.

All the fresh sea air had made
Joshua very tired and soon he was
fast asleep. Mum tucked him up in
bed, then sat outside with Dad and
Emma to watch the sunset.

'It's a shame we have to go home
tomorrow,' said Emma. 'I could stay
here for ever.'

Sheltie gave a long, loud whinny. 'I
think Sheltie agrees,' said Mum,
smiling. 'It *is* beautiful here, isn't it!'

The sun turned into a glowing red
ball and they watched it sink slowly

behind the headland, dissolving into the glimmering sea.

'Come on, it's bedtime,' said Mum. 'We've got to make an early start tomorrow in order to catch the tide.'

'Goodnight, Bird Island,' said Emma. 'Goodnight, Sheltie.' She fell fast asleep as soon as her head hit the pillow.

Chapter Seven

The next morning didn't begin very
well at all. Although Dad had
hammered the tethering peg deep
into the sand, Toby had pulled it out
and wandered off again. Sheltie woke
everyone up by snorting and
whinnying and making a terrible
din.

They all got dressed quickly and
hurried outside to see what the fuss

was about. Then they discovered
what had happened.

'Good boy, Sheltie,' said Emma.
She rubbed his neck hard and turned
to Dad. 'Where could Toby have
gone? You don't think he's crossed
the sands on his own, do you?'

'I hope not,' said Dad. 'I wouldn't
have thought Toby would have
wandered off without Sheltie
anyway.'

'We'd better start searching,' said
Mum. 'He could be anywhere.'

'I bet Sheltie can find him,' said
Emma. 'Sheltie knows where he is,
don't you, boy!'

Sheltie pawed at the sand with his
hoof.

'Tack him up then, Emma,' said

Dad urgently, 'and ride round the island. See if Sheltie can find him. I'll climb the hill and try to spot Toby from up there.'

'And I'll get everything ready here,' said Mum, 'so that we'll be able to go as soon as you find him.'

'*If* we find him,' said Dad. He sounded anxious. 'I just hope he hasn't gone too far.'

'Don't worry, Dad,' said Emma. 'Sheltie will find him.' She put on Sheltie's saddle, tightened his girth and fitted his bridle. Soon Emma was mounted and trotting off with Sheltie around the island.

'Go on, Sheltie,' cried Emma. 'Take me to Toby! You can find him, can't you?'

Sheltie took a deep sniff and blew a confident snort.

They hadn't been going for very long when Sheltie suddenly stopped. A clearing to the left of them opened out between two big sand dunes and led away from the beach into the trees.

Emma held the reins loosely and gave Sheltie his head. Sheltie turned and walked between the dunes into the clearing.

Up ahead the trees formed a big circle, with a carpet of fresh green grass growing in the middle. Behind the trees, where the island began to rise up on to the hill, Emma saw the giant shape of Toby. He was leaning against a thick tree trunk, scratching his shoulders on the rough bark.

Emma noticed that the loose rope attached to Toby's head-collar was tangled in the tree's roots.

'There he is, Sheltie,' said Emma. 'And look, poor Toby's gone and got himself all caught up.'

When Sheltie saw Toby he let out a loud whinny. Toby answered with a series of low snorts and looked over towards Sheltie. Toby seemed really happy to see his little friend.

Emma rode up, then dismounted and untangled Toby's lead rope from the tree roots.

'There!' said Emma as she finally pulled the rope free. 'Come on, Toby. Let's get you back.'

Emma held the lead rope and Toby followed Sheltie back without

protest. He ambled along behind the little pony through the clearing and on to the beach.

'It really is just like leading an elephant, isn't it, Sheltie?' laughed Emma. Sheltie shook out his mane. Emma was sure that he understood what she was saying.

Dad was already back at the

64

caravan. From the top of the hill, he had spotted Emma and Sheltie leading Toby and had raced down to tell Mum.

'If we hurry and get Toby harnessed quickly, we might just make it across the bay before the tide starts to turn,' said Dad.

Sheltie and Emma led the way again and everything was going fine until they were about halfway across the sands.

Suddenly, Toby stopped and the caravan lurched to a halt.

'What's happened?' asked Mum.

'I don't know,' said Dad. He flipped the reins across Toby's neck, but Toby wouldn't move.

'What's the matter with him,

Emma?' said Dad. 'Get Sheltie to make him move.'

'He can't,' said Emma. She was staring down at the caravan wheels.

'Why not? What's happened?' Dad handed the reins to Mum and jumped down.

'The wheels,' said Emma. 'Look at the wheels.'

Dad looked and saw that the caravan's wheels had sunk down into the sand. The lower rims of the back wheels were completely covered. The caravan was well and truly stuck.

Chapter Eight

'We'll have to push,' said Dad. 'All of us at the back, quickly.'

Emma helped too and left Sheltie at the front to encourage Toby.

But it was no good. The wheels began to move, but as soon as Toby felt the dead weight of the caravan, he stopped pulling and the wheels rocked back into their deep grooves.

'Go up front with Sheltie, Emma,'

said Dad, 'and try again to urge Toby forward.'

Emma did, but it was useless. Toby tried his best and pulled as hard as he could. Sheltie coaxed him forward with lots of pony noises. But again, as soon as Toby felt the weight of the caravan behind him, he stopped pulling.

'It's too much for him,' said Dad. 'The caravan's in too deep.'

Then Mum noticed that the tide was coming in. Before, where there had been dry sand, there was now a covering of shimmering water.

'What are we going to do?' said Mum.

'A tractor could pull us out,' suggested Emma.

Dad looked at Mum then turned to Emma.

'Right then, Emma. Can you ride Sheltie as quickly as you can to the mainland and find help? Stop at the farm we passed on the way over. They're bound to have a tractor.'

'I'll be as quick as I can,' said Emma.

She felt really nervous, but she was going to do her best. It wasn't very far to the mainland. They were halfway there already. Emma was determined to bring help.

Emma turned Sheltie's head and set off at a canter towards the mainland on the rescue mission.

The first building Emma came to wasn't a farm at all, but a small

cottage. Emma jumped off Sheltie at the gate, ran with him up the front path and hammered on the door.

There was no answer.

Emma knocked on the door again.

'Please come. Please, please come,' she whispered to herself. But no one

70

did. Sheltie let out a loud whinny. If anyone was at home they would have heard *that*!

Emma ran Sheltie back down the path as the first drops of rain began to fall.

At the gate she jumped into the saddle and Sheltie set off again at a fast trot along the road. Emma had seen another house right at the top of the hill.

'If we can find a way up there, Sheltie, maybe someone will be in this time.'

Sheltie shook the raindrops from his mane and trotted on.

They followed a steep track leading up the hill. The rain was a steady drizzle now, but Emma didn't care.

She noticed marks of tractor wheels deep in the mud and her heart lifted.

'That's what we're looking for, Sheltie. A tractor. A tractor that will pull the caravan out of the sand.'

But the track had stopped suddenly and Emma couldn't see the way up to the house.

Sheltie seemed to know where he was going though. Emma relaxed her hold on the reins and Sheltie walked around a low wall on to a second track. This track led straight up a slope to the house.

The house was a square-built farmhouse. And in the front yard stood a tractor.

'This is the farm Dad saw!' said Emma. Sheltie lifted his head and

snorted loudly. He was as excited as
Emma.

Emma rode Sheltie right up to the
door and hammered on it with all her
strength.

She waited and waited for someone
to answer, but again no one came.
Emma trotted Sheltie round to the
back, but the farm was deserted. There
was nothing but empty barns and
sheds.

'Where is everybody?' said Emma
out loud.

The rain had brought with it a bitter
wind. Emma felt cold and damp. She
shivered as Sheltie glanced round at a
sudden noise. It was the sound of a car
coming along the road below. Emma
stood up in her stirrups. She couldn't

see anything because the road curved away beneath the hill, out of sight – but she could hear the car. And so could Sheltie.

Emma urged Sheltie back down the steep path. She leaned back in the saddle and eased the reins to help Sheltie keep his footing. Then she started to shout for the car to stop.

Sheltie reached the bottom of the

track just as the car sped past. Emma waved and yelled, but the car showed no signs of stopping and disappeared around the bend.

The wind whipped the rain into her face as Emma stared at the empty road in front of them.

'Oh no, Sheltie,' she moaned. 'It's gone.'

Emma guessed that by now the tide would be well on its way in. She thought of Mum, Dad and little Joshua stranded on the sands and choked back her tears.

Then Emma had a thought. If there was one car on the road then there might be another. She rode Sheltie over to the side of the road and waited.

It seemed as if they were there for ages before she saw the next car. It was only a speck in the distance on the long stretch of road. But it was a car. And it was coming their way.

'We've got to stop this car, Sheltie,' said Emma. 'But how?'

Chapter Nine

Emma made Sheltie stand still at the side of the road. But Sheltie was fidgeting and pulling at his reins.

'Don't be frightened,' soothed Emma. 'It'll be all right.'

But Sheltie wasn't frightened. He seemed to want to stand in the middle of the road. That way the car would see them and not go whizzing past. Emma was sure that Sheltie was trying to tell her something and let him move to the middle of the road.

The car roared up. It was now only a few metres in front of them.

Sheltie and Emma were very brave and stood their ground. For a moment it looked as though the car was going to hit them. Emma couldn't bear to look and closed her eyes.

The car screeched to a halt. 'What do you think you are doing?' the driver yelled at Emma.

'I need help,' cried Emma.

Inside the car were the driver and three other people, two women and another man. Emma quickly poured out her story.

'Right!' said the driver. 'You lead
the way and we'll follow.'

The road ended up in a car park at
the edge of the bay. Emma could see
a shallow covering of water lapping
across the stretch of sand ahead. The
tide was taking hold. Then she saw

the caravan, with the sea nearly halfway up its wheels. And Toby's big hoofs and fetlocks were covered by water.

Mum and Dad had lifted as much as they could carry out on to the back steps of the caravan. They had their shoes off and their trousers rolled up. Mum was holding Joshua, who thought it was all a big game.

Dad was just about to unharness Toby and lead him to safety when he heard Emma shouting. He looked up to see Sheltie and Emma galloping towards them, with the rescue party running along behind.

'Well done, Emma!' called Mum. 'You made it just in time.'

'Let's see what a bit of extra weight
will do,' said Dad.

Emma and Joshua sat on Sheltie.
Joshua kept pulling at his own little
riding hat and Emma had to make
him sit still. Everyone else went to
the back of the caravan to push.

'You keep Sheltie at Toby's head,
Emma,' said Dad. 'And get Sheltie to
make Toby pull for all he's worth.'

81

Sheltie put his nose up to Toby's and whickered softly. Toby seemed to understand. And when Sheltie walked away ahead of Toby everyone pushed. Toby strained forward to follow Sheltie and pulled really hard.

'Come on, Toby, you can do it. You can do it,' shouted Emma.

Sheltie whinnied to encourage Toby forward.

'Keep pushing, keep pushing,' yelled Dad. 'It's moving. It's moving!'

Sheltie let out an enormous snort and with one extra effort from Toby the caravan came out of the sand.

'Keep him going, Emma. Don't let him stop,' called Dad. And Sheltie carried on leading Toby forward.

Mum jumped into the driver's seat
and took up the reins.

'Walk on, Toby. Walk on,' Mum

called. And the others followed on behind, cheering and pushing just in case Toby decided to stop.

They kept going steadily and the caravan rolled to the shore with Toby following Sheltie every step of the way. In five minutes they were all safely back on dry sand and crossing to the car park.

Sheltie had done it! He had got Toby to pull the caravan without stopping once.

Dad couldn't thank the driver and his friends enough for coming to their rescue.

'I don't know what we would have done without you,' he said, gratefully.

'It's a good job you had that little

girl of yours and that plucky little pony with you,' said one of the women. Then they said goodbye and went back to collect their car.

It had stopped raining now, but Emma was soaked through to the skin.

She changed into some dry clothes and then they set off to take the caravan back to the farm.

'We're really proud of you, Emma,' Mum said. 'We can always rely on you and Sheltie in an emergency!'

Sheltie puffed out his chest when he heard his name and Emma clapped his neck and gave it a good rub.

When they returned the caravan, Emma told the farmer what had happened. She remembered every detail. Emma wanted to get the story exactly right for when she told Sally. After all, it had turned out to be the most exciting part of the holiday.

Chapter Ten

When they had packed up the car
and it was time to go, Emma
suddenly noticed that Sheltie was
missing. She had left him standing
contentedly on his own next to the
caravan in the middle of the yard.

'Where's Sheltie?' gasped Emma.
After everything that had happened
Emma couldn't bear it if Sheltie had
wandered off and got lost.

Then she heard a familiar snort coming from the caravan and raced round to take a look. Emma suddenly burst out laughing. Sheltie had clambered up the low steps right into the caravan!

The half door had closed behind him, and Sheltie was stood there with his head poking out of the window as though he were in a fancy stable.

'Come and look at Sheltie,' laughed Emma. 'He's made his home in the caravan, just like we did.'

Sheltie's eyes twinkled through his long forelock and he blew a noisy raspberry.

Dad raised his camera and took a snapshot.

'That's one for the album,' he said.

'Sheltie the brave! In a stable fit for a hero!'

And with that, Sheltie grabbed hold of the curtains in his teeth and pretended to eat them. He yanked so hard that the curtains closed.

'Oh, Sheltie,' giggled Emma. 'You are naughty at times. But you're so funny.'

Sheltie stood with his nose poking through the fabric and blew a fanfare of loud snorts.

Even the farmer saw the joke and bellowed like a prize bull.

'I've had all kinds of people come and go in my caravan,' he said. 'But this is the first time I've ever had a pony passenger.'

Sheltie answered with a first-class raspberry and stuck his head through the curtains to take a well-earned bow.